margaret Tempest.

THE STORY OF FUZZYPEG THE HEDGEHOG

BY ALISON UTTLEY
PICTURES BY
MARGARET TEMPEST

LONDON: WILLIAM HEINEMANN LTD.

THE STORY OF FUZZYPEG
THE HEDGEHOG

EARLY ONE SUMMER MORNING, when the white mist lay over the fields like a soft blanket, old Hedgehog uncurled himself and rolled out of bed.

"Don't wake Fuzzypeg," called Mrs Hedgehog, warningly, as he rubbed his bruised shin, and struggled with a sheet which was all mixed up with his prickles.

Hedgehog managed to get unravelled without spoiling the leaf-linen sheet of which Mrs Hedgehog was so proud. He stooped over Fuzzypeg, who lay curled up in bed, a small ball of prickles.

"He'll be a grand fellow when he is grown up," said he to his wife.

OVER THE HEAD OF THE BED hung a string of bobbins, a present from Little Grey Rabbit, who lived in the house on the edge of the Wood, and on the floor lay a poppy-head drum.

Hedgehog went downstairs with his prickles lowered, lest they should brush the whitewash off the ceiling, and walked into the kitchen. Mrs Hedgehog polished him up with a duster, and gave him a clean brown handkerchief.

He opened the door and took down a small wooden yoke, and slung it across his shoulders with the two chains hanging, one on each side.

O N THE HOOKS OF THESE HE hung two little wooden pails, and, hitching them up, he started off to get the milk.

"Don't be late," called Mrs Hedgehog. "Breakfast is at six o'clock today. It is Fuzzypeg's birthday."

The mist was so thick he could scarcely see, but he trotted down the beaten path, through the furze gate, as prickly as himself, into the fields.

He walked straight through the meadow, under a five-barred gate, to another field of short pasture grass. A low deep sound of breathing reached him, and out of the whiteness appeared a herd of cows, dozing as they stood waiting for the sunrise.

"Coo-up, Coo-up," called Hedgehog, and a roan-and-white Cow raised her head and watched him unhook his pails and remove the yoke. Hedgehog gave her a nudge; "Lie down," he commanded, and she obediently lay down.

"There's going to be a fine sunrise this morning," said the Cow.

"How do you know?" said Hedgehog.

"By the clouds, like curds and whey," answered the Cow. "When they are like butter, it will be dull," she continued.

"AND WHAT HAPPENS WHEN THE clouds are like eggs?" asked Hedgehog.

"Then it will rain!" said the Cow.

"Talking of eggs, I shouldn't mind one myself," Hedgehog remarked.

"Plenty in the hen-house," replied the Cow.

Hedgehog milked steadily. The little pails were soon frothing over with milk, so he politely thanked the Cow, and took up his yoke.

Off he walked, with brimming pails, to the house where lived Grey Rabbit and her friends, Hare and Squirrel.

HEDGEHOG KNOCKED AT THE door, and Grey Rabbit opened it.

"You are early this morning, Hedgehog," she said.

"Yes, Grey Rabbit, it is my little Fuzzypeg's birthday," replied the Hedgehog.

"How old is he?" asked Grey Rabbit.

"A year – half-grown up," said the Hedgehog.

"Wait a minute, and I will send him a present," said Grey Rabbit. She came running down with a hen's egg.

"It's a Boiled Egg," she said. "Little Fuzzypeg can play ball with it."

HEDGEHOG THANKED HER AND walked along the lane to Moldy Warp's house. He went to the door and knocked. It opened a crack.

"You are early this morning, Hedgehog," said the Mole.

"It is little Fuzzypeg's birthday to-day," said the Hedgehog.

"Wait a minute and I will send him a present," said the Mole. He came back with a hen's egg. "It's a Scrambled Egg," said he. "I had to scramble under a haystack and back with it."

"Oh, thank you, kind Moldy Warp, Fuzzypeg *will* be pleased."

The Hedgehog walked across the field, and under a stone wall, to an old black house. He knocked at the door and a Rat answered. Hedgehog felt slightly nervous at Rat's house, and never turned his back, although Rat seemed a friendly fellow.

"Here's the milk," said Hedgehog, quickly.

"You're in a hurry," said the Rat.

"Yes, it's my Fuzzypeg's birthday."

"And how old is he?" asked the Rat.

"A YEAR," SAID HEDGEHOG, feeling uneasy.

"I will send him a present," said the Rat. He ran to his cupboard and took out an egg. "It's a Poached Egg," he said solemnly. "I poached it last night from the hen-house."

Hedgehog put it in his bag with the other eggs. "Thank you, Rat," he said.

There was one more house to visit, and that was Red Squirrel's. Hedgehog knocked at the door, and Red Squirrel came tumbling downstairs.

"You are early with the milk, Hedgehog," said he.

"YES," SAID THE HEDGEHOG. "IT is little Fuzzypeg's birthday and I must be quick. He is a year old to-day."

"Your little Fuzzypeg's birthday? I must send him a present," and he ran to the top of the tree. He came down carrying an egg, a dark-brown egg.

"It's an Old-Laid Egg," said he, "the same age as Fuzzypeg."

So Hedgehog put the Old-Laid Egg with the others and hurried home.

"How kind everyone is!" he thought.

Fuzzypeg was sitting on a little chair, waiting for his bread and milk, when Hedgehog arrived.

"ALL THESE PRESENTS ARE FOR Fuzzypeg," said he.

Fuzzypeg had the Scrambled Egg for breakfast, and divided the Poached Egg between father and mother. The Old-Laid Egg and the Boiled Egg he kept for toys.

After breakfast, Hedgehog went out with his son to play "Rolling". They climbed up a hill with the eggs, and rolled down to the bottom.

"Bumpitty Bump!" went Fuzzypeg.

"Bumpitty Bump!" went the Boiled Egg. "Squishitty Squash!" went the Old-Laid Egg.

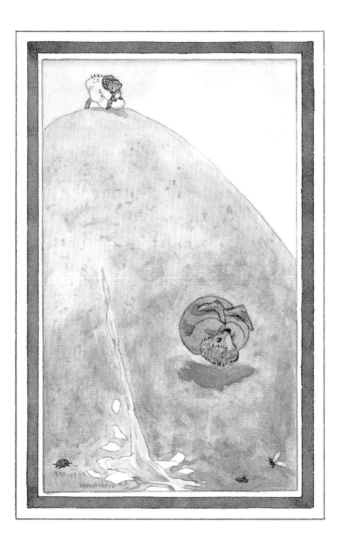

SUCH A SMELL AROSE! HEDGEHOG and Fuzzypeg took to their heels and ran all the way home.

When evening came and the sun went down in a sea of gold, Hedgehog gave Fuzzypeg his present – a green parcel.

Fuzzypeg opened it with trembling paws. Inside was a little white cage, made of the pith of rushes. Two small black creatures lay within.

As he held the cage, twilight came, and the little creatures sent out a beautiful soft light, so that the cage was like a fairy lantern.

"WHAT ARE THEY?" ASKED Fuzzypeg.

"Glow-worms," replied Hedgehog. "Two tame glow-worms. Feed them and treat them kindly, and then you can let them loose in the hedge-garden."

Fuzzypeg hung up the cage from a hook in the ceiling, and the room was filled with the delicate light. But when he came down the next day, the glow-worms were fast asleep, and so they remained till evening.

Hedgehog was very fond of eggs, and began to poach, but usually he found nothing, for Rat had been there first.

Then, on a lovely September day, he had a great adventure. He was strolling through the fields, holding Fuzzypeg's hand, when suddenly the hens began to cry and hiss and scream.

"Help! Help! Help! Save us! Run for your life!" they cried as they rushed to the shelter of the farm.

All except a Speckledy Hen, who was too frightened to move. She stood staring at an adder, which glided nearer and nearer.

Fuzzypeg trembled and stayed very still, but Hedgehog sprang at the adder's tail, and held it with teeth and hands.

OVER AND OVER AGAIN THE adder tried to bite Hedgehog, but Old Hedgehog never let go until the adder lay dead.

The Speckledy Hen said, shaking, "Hedgehog, you saved my life."

"It's nothing. Pray don't mention it," said Hedgehog, modestly. "It's months since I tasted Hadder Pie. My wife will be glad of this," and he slung the adder across his back, and went home with the admiring Fuzzypeg.

AFTER A FINE DINNER OF ADDER Pie, Fuzzypeg ran out to play with his cousins, Tim and Bill Hedgehog.

"I say!" said he, "My father killed a Nadder! He pounced on it and held its tail till it was dead."

"That's nothing," said Bill Hedgehog, scornfully. "My father pounced on a Lion's tail and held it till it was dead!"

Fuzzypeg ran in and out of the slender trees, pretending to enjoy himself, but his heart was heavy. "I don't want to play to-day," he said, and he walked home to his father and his mother through the bracken.

"MOTHER," SAID HE, "IF MY father met a Lion, could he pounce on its tail and hold tight till it was dead?"

"Of course he could," replied Mrs Hedgehog, looking up from her sewing, and old Hedgehog proudly rattled the milk pail, and wisely said nothing.

"He could fight an elephant, I expect," said Fuzzypeg to himself. "Tell me the tale of how Grey Rabbit killed the Weasel," he implored his mother.

He made up his mind to be very brave like his father and Grey Rabbit.

Every morning the grateful Speckledy Hen laid an egg under the Sycamore tree, and every day Mrs Hedgehog divided it neatly into three parts, for Hedgehog, Fuzzypeg and herself. She wanted to repay the kindness of the Hen, so one day she made a hay-seed cake.

"Take this to the Speckledy Hen," she said to Fuzzypeg. "Do not dawdle on the way home. Walk on the little green path under the hedge-row, not on the broad white road across the fields. There are dangers about – Weasels, Stoats, Snakes, and worse."

"WHAT SHALL I DO IF I MEET A Danger?" asked Fuzzypeg.

"Roll up in a ball, and keep your face hidden."

"Suppose I meet a lion?"

His mother laughed, "You won't meet a Lion," said she.

He trotted through the fields, picking a few mushrooms and blackberries. He sniffed at the honeysuckle, far above his head, and admired the red rose-hips. When he got to the Low Meadow he met the Speckledy Hen.

"Mother sent you a hay-seed cake," said he, "and thanks you for the eggs."

"HOW DELICIOUSLY SWEET IT smells!" said the Hen. "Now come with me and I will show you where the finest acorns fall."

She took him to an old oak tree, and he picked up the young acorns.

By the time he started home it was getting late. The blackbirds were calling, "Hurry up, hurry up," to their children, and the thrush was practising her music for next day's wood-concert.

"Stop and play a minute," said Hare.

Fuzzypeg stopped a minute, and a minute more, whilst the Hare tried to explain noughts and crosses to him.

"'WARE STOAT! 'WARE STOAT!"
cawed a rook, as he turned
again for home. He would go along the
white path, he decided.

He hurried along the broad road,
thinking of his supper. Suddenly he saw
a great, white, curly-haired animal.

He hesitated, and the animal saw him.
It roared, and sprang towards him with
frightful springs.

"A Lion," thought poor Fuzzypeg,
and he curled himself up in a ball.

The Lion bounced into him, and got a
bunch of prickles in his nose.

"Bow-Wow! Bow-Wow! Ow! Ow!! Ow!!!" roared the Lion, and he turned and ran to – Oh! Horrors! Fuzzypeg saw a great Elephant advancing.

"Good Dog, Spot; keep off him!" cried a voice.

"Look what Spot and I found, Daddy! A young Hedgehog!"

"Put it in the garden, Tommy; it will catch slugs."

"No, I won't, I *won't* catch slugs!" squeaked Fuzzypeg. "Let me go home. My father is a great Hedgehog, and he once killed a Lion."

TOMMY TOOK NO NOTICE, BUT carried the Hedgehog to the garden, and put him on the path. Slowly Fuzzypeg uncurled and had a peep. Then he bolted for the gate, but he was not quick enough, for Tommy seized him, and put him under an enormous flower-pot. He brought him a bowl of bread and milk, and left him for the night.

WHEN NO LITTLE HEDGEHOG came home, old Hedgehog went out to look for him, along the green lanes and byways. He traced him to the field where he had met the Hare, and on the ground there he found a little paper with O's and X's. Hedgehog could not read it, so he put it in his pocket, and followed the track along the white path. A bundle of acorns tied up in a tiny dirty handkerchief lay there, some mushrooms in a dock-leaf, and a pair of red shoes.

As he examined these, he felt a pair of eyes staring at him, and, turning, he saw the Stoat in the hedge.

Old Hedgehog never knew how he got home to his wife. He was in despair as he showed her the shoes and the pathetic little bundles. But Mrs Hedgehog would not give in.

"You must go this very night to Grey Rabbit's House to ask if they know anything," she said. So Hedgehog set off again, under the golden moon.

He knocked at the door, and Squirrel answered.

"No, we don't want any milk to-night, thank you," said she, shutting the door.

"Please, ma'am, it's my little Fuzzypeg, he's lost."

"DOES ANYONE KNOW WHERE Fuzzypeg Hedgehog is?" she called into the house.

Grey Rabbit came running with a half-knitted sock in her paws, and Hare came with a little green book he was reading.

"I've seen him," said Hare. "We met in the Low Meadow, and we had a little game of noughts and crosses. He will be quite good at it if he practises."

Hedgehog took the paper from his pocket.

"Yes, that's it," said Hare.

"What happened then?" asked Hedgehog.

"HE JUST RAN ON AND ON, AND I ran the other way."

Grey Rabbit then spoke. "I am so sorry, Hedgehog. I advise you to see Wise Owl."

"Wise Owl? Oh no, not Wise Owl!" cried Hedgehog.

"Why not?"

"Because," Hedgehog hesitated, "he might be hungry, you see."

"If you wave a white handkerchief for a truce, you will be safe," said Squirrel.

Little Grey Rabbit tied two white handkerchiefs to his prickles, and he went into the great Wood.

WISE OWL WAS OUT HUNTING when Hedgehog rang the silvery bell on the door of the old oak tree. So he sat down to wait, feeling very small and lonely. High up among the pointed leaves he could see the kindly Moon. He crept closer to the tree, and held his nose against the rough warm bark. It was comforting.

"Too-Whit, Too-Whoo," came nearer and nearer, and Wise Owl, who had heard the bell far away, flew to his house, carrying something which Hedgehog preferred not to see.

"Who are you?" he asked.

"I'm Hedgehog the Milkman, Sir."

"What do you want?"

"Please, Sir, I've lost my little Hedgehog, and Grey Rabbit thought you could find him for me."

The Owl was flattered. "Perhaps I can," he replied, "but I must be paid."

"Anything you like," said Hedgehog.

"Well," said Wise Owl, considering, "I will have a quill for a pen and a can of milk, and a new-laid egg. Bring them to-morrow at dawn, and you shall have news of your son."

Hedgehog thanked him and went home.

WISE OWL FLEW WITH WIDE sweeping wings over the fields looking for little Hedgehog, but nowhere could he see him.

"Stoat, have you seen little Hedgehog?" he asked a shifty-eyed fellow, creeping along the hedges with a club in his hand.

"No, Sir," said Stoat. "I only saw Milkman Hedgehog a moment."

"If you see him, report to me," said Wise Owl, sternly.

"Yes, Sir," said Stoat, touching his slouched hat. "I wish I had seen him," he muttered when Wise Owl had flown away.

"RAT, HAVE YOU SEEN LITTLE Hedgehog?" the Owl asked a dark poacher, creeping under a wall with a twisty wire in his hand.

"No, Sir. I sent him an egg for his birthday, but I've not seen him."

"Report to me if you do," said Wise Owl.

"Yes, Sir," said the Rat, touching his cap, and hurrying on.

"Yard-dog, have you seen little Hedgehog?" the Owl asked a curly white dog, sitting outside his kennel, singing to the moon.

"Yes," answered the dog, "I've seen him, but I shall tell you nothing about him. I belong to the House, and you belong to the Wood," and the dog proudly shook his chain.

"He must be somewhere near," thought the Owl, so he searched the lawn and pigsty, and the orchard.

A little sound caught his keen ears, as he flew slowly over the garden, a sound of weeping and soft sobbing.

"Mother, Mother, Grey Rabbit, Father, Moldy Warp. Come! Come! Oh! I'm so lonely and lost!"

THE SOUNDS CAME FROM A large inverted flower-pot, standing firmly in the rhubarb bed. The Owl flew down and looked through the hole in the top.

The sobbing ceased, for little Fuzzypeg was terribly alarmed to see a bright eye instead of the far cluster of stars.

"Is that you, little Hedgehog?" asked the Owl.

"Yes, it's me," said the little creature, trembling.

"Help is coming," said the Owl, and he flew away home, for his work was over.

A T DAWN CAME THE HEDGEHOG carrying a can of milk, a goose-quill for a pen, and a new-laid egg. He rang the bell and waved the handkerchiefs. Owl, who was just getting ready for bed, looked through the door.

"Put them down there, Hedgehog. Your son is safe under a flower-pot in the farmer's garden."

Hedgehog thanked him and started home at a run, calling on his way for Little Grey Rabbit, Hare, Squirrel and Moldy Warp. Mrs Hedgehog ran to the door when she heard the patter of little feet, and she joined them.

THEY ALL RAN THROUGH THE fields, Hare and Little Grey Rabbit leading, Squirrel coming next . . . .

Hedgehog and Mrs Hedgehog panting after . . . .

. . . . and Moldy Warp far behind.

They squeezed under the gate (except the fat Hare, who had to climb the wall), and ran across the lettuces and carrots, down the little path between the gooseberry bushes, to the red rhubarb, where stood an enormous plant-pot.

"ARE YOU THERE, FUZZYPEG?" called old Hedgehog.

"Yes, Father, are you?" answered a small faint voice.

"Yes, we are all here," said Hedgehog; "Squirrel, Hare and Grey Rabbit, and Moldy Warp is on the way."

He turned to the animals. "All push, and over the plant-pot must go."

So they pushed and they pushed, but the plant-pot didn't move.

"Steady, boys! Now! All together! SHOVE!!" called Hedgehog, but still the plant-pot did not move.

A LARGE RAT STROLLED UP. "What are you doing?" said he.

"Little Hedgehog is under this plant-pot," explained Hedgehog.

"Oh, he's found, is he? But you will never move that thing if Hare pushes one way and you all push the other. Now, heave ho!!!" shouted Rat, but as they all pushed away from him, the plant-pot still did not move.

They stuck their little feet in the ground, and puffed and panted and bumped their shoulders. Little Hedge-hog inside shouted, "Push harder! Push harder!"

THEN MOLDY WARP TURNED UP.
"Not that way," said he,
quietly. "If the pot fell over, you would
all be squashed. This is the way."

He planted his feet firmly, and with
nose and hands dug rapidly into the soil
by the flower-pot. Earth flew in a shower,
and in a few seconds he disappeared
down the tunnel he had made. The
animals waited.

Then a tiny snout appeared, and little
Hedgehog crawled up the tunnel, to be
hugged, prickles and all, by old

Hedgehog and his wife. A minute later came Mole, wiping his lips.

"I stopped to finish his bread and milk," he explained. "It was a pity to waste it."

He rammed the soil down in the tunnel, and the happy procession started home.

"Don't forget to tell Wise Owl that I found little Hedgehog," called the Rat.

"Come into the garden and have some refreshments," said Mrs Hedgehog, when they got back.

HEDGEHOG AND MRS HEDGEHOG brought egg sandwiches, acorns baked in their skins, rose-hip jam, fresh blackberries and cream, mushrooms on toast, and crab-apple cider.

When the Hare, the Squirrel, and the Little Grey Rabbit went home, they each took a small quill pen, which the grateful Hedgehog had made for them; but Moldy Warp wouldn't have anything. He said digging was more in his line than writing, and he had everything he wanted in his castle under the Ten-Acre field.

William Heinemann Ltd
Michelin House
81, Fulham Road, London SW3 6RB

LONDON · MELBOURNE · AUCKLAND

Text and illustrations copyright © William Heinemann 1932
First published 1932
This edition published 1992
ISBN 434 96926 5
Produced by Mandarin
Printed and bound in Hong Kong